Doctor Foster
went to Gloucester

Retold by Russell Punter

Illustrated by David Semple

Reading consultant: Alison Kelly
Roehampton University

Doctor Foster went
to Gloucester,

in a shower of rain.

He stepped in a puddle,

right up to his middle,

and never went
there again.

Doctor Foster went
to Oxford,

in a cloud of fog.

He just couldn't see,

bumped into a tree

and splat! He fell
into a bog.

Doctor Foster went
to Gosport,

in a howling gale.

The wind was so strong,

it blew him along,

and he flew down the street with a wail.

Wooo*aaaaa!*

Doctor Foster went
to Stockton,

in the swirling snow.

The frost bit his nose,

his spectacles froze

and he couldn't see
which way to go.

Doctor Foster went
to Bognor,

in the sizzling heat.

He took off his socks,

fell asleep on
some rocks

and got sunburned all
over his feet.

Doctor Foster
told his daughter,

"I'm not going to roam."

"I'll see patients here,

with my family near."

"From now on, there's
no place like home."

PUZZLES

Puzzle 1

Can you spot the differences between these two pictures? There are six to find.

Puzzle 2
Match the weather to the picture.

wind   fog   rain   snow

1.

2.

3.

4.

Puzzle 3
Find these things in
the picture.

cat   hat   bird   bag

puddle   cloud

Answers to puzzles

Puzzle 1

Puzzle 2

1.
snow

2.
rain

3.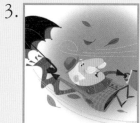
wind

4.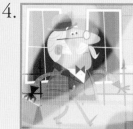
fog

Puzzle 3

cloud

hat

bag

puddle   cat   bird

About the rhyme

The original version of *Doctor Foster* appeared in 1810. The rhyme we know today was first published in 1844. Some people think it is about Edward I of England (1239-1307). There is a story that, on a visit to Gloucester, he fell off his horse into a puddle and swore he would never return.

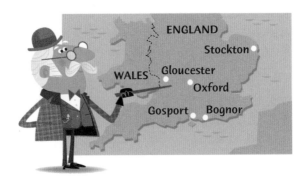

Series editor: Lesley Sims

First published in 2012 by Usborne Publishing Ltd., Usborne House, 83-85 Saffron Hill, London EC1N 8RT, England. www.usborne.com
Copyright © 2012 Usborne Publishing Ltd.